Moments of the Heart II

Carolyn Dunn Hagan

ok online at www.trafford.com
rs@trafford.com

l titles are also available at major online book retailers.

arians: A cataloguing record for this book is available from Library
Canada at www.collectionscanada.ca/amicus/index-e.html

toria, BC, Canada.

4269-1631-1(sc)
4269-1632-8 (hc)

ngress Control Number: 2009935522

s to efficiently provide the world's finest, most comprehensive book publishing
ing every author to experience success. To find out how to publish your book, your
e it available worldwide, visit us online at www.trafford.com

09/21/09

fford
LISHING®   www.trafford.com
ca & international

Moments of
the Heart II

Carolyn Dunn Hagan

I have been blessed with 2 beautiful children

I have put these poems together to leave for them.

My daughter Shannon

and

My Son Derek

The sunshine of my life!

Carolyn Dunn Hagan

1951 –

Arlington, Texas

Moments of the heart, captured on paper.

If one poem, one verse, or even one line

should touch the heart of another,

then it was worth the writing.

The pictures within this book are all my own as photography ha
my hobby, as well as writing poems, crocheting dolls, racing my
Am and playing softball.

Contents

A Whisper ....

Always There ....

Beside Me ....

Big Bend Trip ....

Brighter Day ....

Daybreak ....

Do or Don't ....

Dreaming ....

End of A Season ....

Footprints ....

From the Start ....

Give me Strength ....

Goodbye ....

Grandma and Grandpa Too ....

Harley or a Horse ....

Harley or a Horse …continued ....

Hear my Prayer ....

Heartaches ....

Hello ....

His Guiding Light ....

Home ....

Humble Knock ....

Hummingbirds ....

I Love My Job ....

I Remember ....

If I Could ....

In Need ....

I've Seen ....

in...46

Song...47

s On 49

ime...51

ad Traveled 52

....54

....56

....57

d Fibber McGee 59

t Filled..60

hine...63

t Boy 64

....65

es 67

Never Know 69

....70

....71

Moments 73

Passing Moment 74

....77

l Beneath the Shield..78

Life 79

....80

o our Heart..83

ant Light 84

night Hour 87

st of a Storm 88

ning's Dawn...90

....93

m Passes By 94

ey Were Grown   96

Tokens ....

Unto You ....

Values ....

What a Difference ....

What Jesus Said ....

When ....

When I Fall Silent ....

Will You ....

Who ....

Words ....

World of Beauty ....

Yesterday ....

Young Once ....

A Whisper

When love steps quietly by
With hardly even a whisper
Let not the embers die
Or morning air the crisper

So much to say, but yet unspoken
Leaves one to wonder why
And all the hopeful dreams are broken
And a heart that's left to sigh

Set aside those hopes and dreams
Now only to remember
Memories are all that's left it seems
Of that fire lit warmth of December

Always There

He's always there beside me

No matter what I do

Even when I'm working

He's there the whole day through

He's with me when I'm walking

The fields far and wide

He never leaves for a moment

And is always by my side

He's there when I am lonely

And must go on my own

He lets me know he's with me

By the little ways he's shown

And when troubles are too heavy

He takes me by the hand

I don't leave home without him

Beside Me

Who will walk beside me
As we travel from day to day
And together gain great pleasure
In the things we do and say

Who will stand beside me
Whenever things go wrong
And offer me some comfort
And help me to be strong

Who will sit beside me
When I am old and gray
And talk about old memories
To pass the time of day

Who will be beside me
As I reach my journey's end
Will it be a stranger

Big Bend Trip

A friend and I took a trip to Big Bend

I thought the days would never end

I learned when they say 'Hey, Trust Me!

Beware of what else there might be to see

There were horses to ride all the day long

And mountains to climb, so one had to be strong!

We didn't eat until daylight had passed

I wasn't sure if my strength would last.

Then we ran out of gas and took the short cut,

Like someone before us that built an old hut.

Forced to excitement that gave a big chill,

We walked among flowers in Rattlesnake Hills!

Then climbed a mountain to an old abandoned cave

But with no bears or lions, we looked so brave!

Then finally, to relax we took a raft downstream,

But when the guide found the rapids, I had to scream

Now, looking back, I'm sure we had fun,

Brighter Day

If I could only brighten
Someone's lonely day
Or make someone smile
Somewhere along the way

If all I had to offer
Was time with one to share
Or maybe some small token
Just to show I care

If I could only add
A fraction of delight
It might make one's burdens
Seem a little bit more light

Daybreak

What light shines upon the window sill

And gives breath of life to the morning still

Wakened now to the sounds of Spring

As birds unite and begin to sing

The tall oak trees begin to sway

In the gentle breeze that starts the day

What forbids me from my slumber

It's quick to see, I am outnumbered

The hours few, so quickly pass

Before shadows fall upon the glass

Do or Don't

Caught between do or don't
Can tear one apart
The choices don't come easy
And can play upon the heart

I found out that it's when I do
It had better be what's right
For if I should've went with don't
It could sometimes cause a fight

Then there's don'ts, at times should do
And boy the trouble starts
So I found that when I'm given a choice
Just do what's right from the heart

Then there's times, it matters not
Neither do or don't can't win
Oh, to know the choice to make

Dreaming

Should we live in the moment

Or live for days to come

If we find that true perfection

They both would become one

Looking out the windows

For one to share a dream

And together keep on dreaming

And gently spread our wings

Maybe I am a dreamer

But I know there'll come a chance

One day there'll be a moment

And together we will dance

So, I'll just keep on dreaming

Until the day I find

The height to all the purpose

End of A Season

Love is not lost at the end of a season

Continue to hold it dear

Come one day, you'll see the reason

When all your loved ones gather near

When a tear shall fill your eyes no more

And light shall never go dim

Time shall cease past Heaven's door

And to God, we give praise unto him

We'll hear the sound of angelic song

And see Heaven's awesome glow

We'll see the face of who rights the wrong

And through faith, all Christians know

So hold fast the heartfelt love

Keep memories within the heart

Comfort comes on a white winged dove

Footprints

I gazed across the forest timbers
With leaves of autumn gold
Dew upon the grasses glimmer
As thoughts of past unfold

Who walked this path years ago
Whose footprints mark this land
Who lived, who died, who came to know
This spot on which I stand

Of those past, whose spirits lay
Their word shall prevail
As clouds part in the sky one day
And on angels wings they sail

Glory Hallelujah

Thank God their story was told

I want to go when the clouds roll back

And see those streets of gold

Glory Hallelujah

Thank God their story reached me

I'm ready to sail without fail

And Jesus I shall see

From the Start

You were always there
Ever since I've been me
Watching and waiting
For your love I would see

When I would fall
You were always so near
Now that I'm older
I can see more clear

You would pick me up
When I was down
And make a smile
Wipe away the frown

I loved you then
Right from the start
And I love you now

Give me Strength

Oh, the pain that fills my heart
As I watch you grow weary and weak

Now is the time I must do my part
Though tears make it hard to speak

I must be strong and take the lead
For now you must lean on me

So to my Father, my heart does plead
For strength from bended knee

Goodbye

The birds hushed their singing
And Mama wiped her eyes
God opened up his gate
When Papa said 'Goodbye'

The angels gathered round
And welcomed Papa in
They said 'Come with us'
And Papa gave a grin

Years passed since Papa left
And Mama was never the same
She had left Papa's favorite slippers
Beside his chair and walking cane

Now Mama's health is failing

As she sits in Papa's chair

She too will soon be leaving

To that land so bright and fair

The house now seems empty

And memories are all that remain

But if you listen, you'll hear a whisper

'For them, God will do the same'

Grandma and Grandpa Too

We could hear the birds singing

Their old familiar song

And as grandma did the dishes

She whistled right along

She cooked the best fried chicken

And made the best sweet tea

And when I'd come to visit

She'd cook a lot for me

Oh, how I loved my grandma

And loved my grandpa too

Someday when I get older

I want to be just like you

Now grandma read the bible

Then we'd sing a song or two

And as grandpa sat us on his knee

He said 'Always remember child,

Before you sleep, to pray

That Jesus fills your heart with love

And light along your way!'

Oh, how I loved my grandma

And loved my grandpa too

Someday when I have grandkids

I want to be just like you

Harley or a Horse

Which is better, a Harley or a horse?
I'm not too sure of the answer
With both, you need to hold on of course
Especially, on the one called 'Faster'

High in the saddle, Whoohoo look at me,
Riding the wild frontier!
When all of a sudden, a low hanging tree
Just ripped my hand of it's beer!

Whoa! Stop! Turn around quick!
A three second roll at best
Before it all spills, watch this trick
I'll put this stunt to a test!

I leaned way over and began to reach

With awesome style and grace

Then all of a sudden, I looked up ahead

And that tree was in my face!

Forget the beer, come pick me up,

Cause I hit that tree with such force!

When I get well, I'll buy me a Harley

And forget that dumb old horse!

Harley or a Horse ...continued

Some time later......

Well, I bought me a Harley, like I said I would

But I'm not too sure it's for the better

Before I could ride, I had to take a test,

So I followed the rules to the letter!

I bought me some leather and stuff to match

So I'm all geared up for the 'Ride'

I checked the tires and oil and such

And it just filled my heart up with pride!

I looked so cool, that I planned a trip

Confident that I had the skill

But my instructor said 'Hey, listen up!

You gotta give it gas at will'

Well, somehow it seems I got off balance

And went zigzagging down the road

'Just hang on tight and let off the gas

You'll come to a stop' I was told.

Well, hang on I did, my knuckles were white

It scared the devil out of me!

Come to a stop? Well, yes he was right!

Cause someone had planted a TREE!

Now when I get well, this bike's for sale

I wonder what else there could be?

I'll never wonder 'Harley or Horse'

Because neither was right for me!

Hear my Prayer

Oh Father, hear my prayer

For your touch is what I need

To guide my path before me

That I might take some heed

I need some special wisdom

For words in which to sow

So others might come to Jesus

And see heaven and all it's glow

Shower your goodness upon me

So you will receive the glory

As some lost soul might see the light

As they hear your beautiful story

Build me with the confidence

To live no more in shame

Fill me with the knowledge

To glorify your name

And as you hear my prayer, oh Lord

I pray you'll be forgiving

As we break the binding chains of sin

And make a new life worth living

Heartaches

It matters not

What road I take

If you only knew

How my heart aches

How hard I try

To do the best I can

For just a kind word

Or a loving hand

I want to be close

But nothing seems right

Even when I try

With all my might

Yet when I leave

And look back at you

Through bittersweet tears

Hello

From the moment I first saw you

You had me at 'Hello'

I felt a rush flow through me

That reached down to my soul

You took my very heart

And claimed it for your own

I thought I loved you then

But through the years it's grown

This love will last forever

I know it must be so

I was captured with your smile

That moment you said 'Hello'

His Guiding Light

God's plan is beyond what we can fathom

But I know we'll one day see

For in due time we'll see the light

When he calms our troubled sea

As we travel the road before us

Faith is our hope and key

And we pray he'll show his mercy

As we bow on bended knee

Home

There's a place where you can go
When life seems to get you down
A place that's warm and cozy
And heartfelt love abounds

There's a place where you can go
When the pace is hard to keep
A place where you can lay your head
And close your eyes to sleep

There's a place where you can always go
Even though now your grown
This place you knew as a child
And can always call your home

Humble Knock

Wherefore art thou, my Lord and God
Hast thou hidden thy face from me
I pray ye show thy goodness and mercy
As I a sinner bow before thee

I humble myself before thee oh Lord
And from the pit of my heart and soul
I ask for some sign of assurance
That my faith has made me whole

No longer to tread in darkness
But to follow thy glorious light
To see thy path before me
And lead others so they also might

Straighten the path before me oh Lord
That I may falter no more
And do thy works by thy guiding hand

Hummingbirds

Some are like a hummingbird

Never to be still

Do they ever capture a moment

And view it to be real

Just for a second

You'll see them stop in flight

To see the beauty of a heart

That is within their sight

It doesn't go unnoticed

The little things they do

Wondering if they'll ever slow

Or scurry their whole life through

I Love My Job

So many long hours and so much work

Was leaving me at my wits end

So for my good health, I finally got up

And prayed my legs would still manage to bend

I went outside, took a deep breath

And listened to the bird's cheerful song

When what to my wonder, suddenly I heard

Gunshots and knew something was wrong

Wasting no time, I scurried back in

Thinking they were shooting at me

So back to the grind, the harder I worked

Refreshed as I ever could be

Adrenaline flowing, my heart was pounding

As I worked at a most hurried pace

Thank God for my job, no more to complain

I Remember

I remember when you would hold me tight
And before I'd sleep, we said a prayer at night

I remember when you would tuck me in
And kiss my cheek before dreams would begin

I remember when you would hold my hand
Protect me from harm and beside me stand

I remember when you would push my swing
I loved you more than anything

I remember you said how sad you would be
If anything should ever happen to me

I remember when we both would cry
When it came the time to say goodbye

I don't remember you saying what to do

If I Could

If I could

I would ease your pain

Make the sun shine

And take away the rain

If I could

I would say the right words

And fill your world

With flowers and birds

If I could

I would tread all the miles

Just to brighten your day

And to see that cute smile

If I could

I would give you a part

Of the hugs overflowing

In Need

You could see I needed prayer
So you came and touched my hand
Prayed the Lord would intercede
And give me strength to stand

You saw I had a need
You stayed so you could share
Wiped the tears from my eyes
And showed how much you care

Some day when you need prayer
I'll come and hold your hand
Pray the Lord will intercede
And give you strength to stand

When you should have a need
I'll come so I can share
Wipe the tear from your eyes

I've Seen

I've seen those, quick to anger

And some who stand so tall

I've seen the dark clouds hover

And I've seen their empires fall

I've seen those, slow to anger

And seen the humble bow

I've seen their aura shining

And peace upon their brow

I've seen those, way too busy

That they never stop to think

Where will they go when life's over

For it could end with just a blink

I've seen those, try not to falter

As they humbly bow to pray

And live their life for Jesus

Journey

High above the universe

Flew a tiny little bird

He spread his wings like an eagle

When the angel's voice he heard

Higher than the treetops

On his path he flew

Wind nor rain could stop him

As closer to the clouds he drew

Nothing could deter him

Though storms would surely test

At times he grew so weary

That he had to stop and rest

Each 7th day of flying

He stopped for strength to gain

But with heart and mind in focus

On his path he would remain

Nothing could prevent him

For he would not see defeat

For he had such a vision

Of when the Master he would meet

Just Begun

I've just begun to know you
Yet I've known of you for so long
I never even realized
This feeling could be so strong

I was blind and did not see
The things you had in store
Now that I've come to know you
I'm wanting to know you more

Life is a Song

Life is a song

The tune is played each day

Attitude makes the tempo

The pace leads the way

Music hits the heart

The melody sets the tone

If Jesus is the rhythm

Your song will be known

Life Goes On

Life goes on, in endless singing
A song that echoes in my heart
The memories are never ending
Of which my soul could never part

If my weakness should be put to test
With all of earth's creations
My heart would sing at it's best
The memory of love's sensation

And when I draw my last of breath
My heart will continue to singeth
For love never ends, even in death
And shall forever ringeth

Lost in Time

Lost in the time of day
Where I could forever linger
Caring not this way or that
Or even to lift a finger

Caught in a mystic realm
Of thoughts of days gone by
Times that can be no more
And leaves one's heart to sigh

But all too soon, the hands of time
Come to break the slumber
Forced to tend to things at hand
As duties come in numbers

Long Road Traveled

Long, the road of which I've traveled

A familiar path I know

Yet all too quickly comes unraveled

When it's covered up with snow

Hasten the step for light to see

Is quickly going dim

And yet the miles for which to be

Is far to yonder rim

The step I take is quite a test

Knowing not where it leads

And yet to know what is best

I pray I will succeed

What course shall be the lesser grief

When spring melts the snow

For solid ground is such relief

Of which I like to know

The sun shall set and rise tomorrow

And I must do so too

May it brighten the day and end the sorrow

And warm the heart some too

Love

I climbed high upon a mountain
To watch the setting sun
I wished that you were with me
As another day was done

I sat alone there on that mountain
And observed the distant lights
All my thoughts then turned to you
As I heard a song play in the night

A melody so sweetly ringing
Then came thoughts of me with you
And then I wished upon a star
I wished that you could be there too

Then as this day came to a close

It seemed to also bring a tear

For as I lay me down to sleep

I wished that I could hold you near

Did you ever know how much I love you?

Did you ever know how much I care?

Do you ever wish upon a star?

Do you ever wish that I was there?

Loved

The time has come for us to part

As tears stream down our face

But in our sadness there is also joy

In knowing there's a better place

Some sweet day we all shall gather

Where parting will be no more

Then our joy will be complete

As we walk that golden shore

So as we part, you must know

You are loved, as you loved me

And until the time we all shall gather

In my heart, you will always be

Loving

To be loved and be called loving!

To dance within the heart

To a rhythm gently swayed

Knowing not from where it starts

Promising only endless days

Let not the music falter

Let not the melody fade

Reaching heights beyond the measure

Like a tune that's been well played

To be loved and be called loving!

Molly and Fibber McGee

I have no grandkids, because my kids aren't marrie

But I have some grand puppies that must be carriec

Now who has the time to carry a silver platter?

But, Fibber thinks he's king and it really shouldn't ma

Then there's the Queen and her name is Molly

And if she gets out the door, she just looks so jolly,

As she runs down the street, she barks 'Look, I'm Fre

And thinks it's a game and says 'Come chase me!'

Now on the other hand, Fibber looks at me

And if I'm not coming, then neither is he!

If they should hear a noise, there seems to be a choi

As they all bark at once, at any given hour!

Now I'd have an issue, if they weren't so darn cute

When they get in the trash, I'd give 'em a boot

But Fibber's just as close, as I am to he

And Molly's just as cute as she can be!

I guess we'll keep Molly and Fibber McGee

My Heart Filled

I woke to the sound of children at play

For the window was open wide

I rose to look and at a glance

My heart filled up with pride

There sat a boy no older than ten

That looked a lot like me

So intent as he read his book

In the shade of the old oak tree

I combed my hair and went outside

To sit beside the boy

He said 'I love you' and hugged my neck

And my heart filled up with joy

What book do you read with such intent

I asked at the moment's thought

He said the one that I had given

And the only one he'd brought

This book he said holds the answer

About God and heaven above

He said someday we'll all live in heaven

And my heart filled up with love

My Sunshine

You are a special person
I can see it in your eyes
And all the little things you do
Come as no real surprise

You have a special heart
It shows in every way
In the love you show so freely
And in all the things you say

You have a special smile
That seems to make you glow
The world is a brighter place
With someone like you to know

(my daughter, Shannon)

My Sweet Boy

I remember when you were born
A mother's pride and joy
I loved you and I rocked you
My precious little boy

I watched as you went out to play
And discover things on your own
And hoped through the teenage years
You'd not forget the love we've shown

And now that you are older
And quite a handsome man
I'll always call you my sweet boy
Because this mother can

Noticed

What if I had noticed
Each time you noticed me
Each time you touched my arm
And gave up time for me

What if I had noticed
Each time you noticed me
The time you kissed my cheek
And each hug you gave to me

What if I had noticed
That you had noticed too
Each time I touched your arm
Or needed time with you

What if I had noticed

That you had noticed too

That day that you were looking

And I was looking too

What if I had noticed

And know you noticed too

Would it make a difference

Would you turn my light off too

Old Times

I miss old times

You were all mine

By my side

I miss your touch

Loved you so much

You loved me

Life goes on now

On my own now

Since you're gone

Times I feel blue

I still love you

Til I die

One May Never Know

One may never know

Whose heart they may touch

Or in whose life

They have meant so much

One may never know

That with just a smile

Has made someone's life

Seem more worthwhile

One may never know

When what they may say

Has changed someone's life

Or just brightened their day

One may never know

Just by doing a good deed

Has met someone's wish

Peace

Standing high upon a mountain
I watched the setting sun
I felt a brush of gentle breeze
As another day was done

I stood upon that mountain
And watched the distant lights
My heart will forever remember
A song that echoed in the night

A melody sweetly ringing
Throughout the cool crisp air
Just a subtle reminder
That God is always there

When this day came to a close
All my cares released
And as I lay down to sleep

People

Countless faces that we meet

Knowing not what lies beneath

Hurried the pace for time to keep

For duties that call before they sleep

What thoughts are kept behind those eyes

Leaves one to wonder and only surmise

There is a clue in the way they walk

Or if you listen to the way they talk

Do they gesture with their hand

Do they bend or is straight their stand

The secrets within, we may not know

But intriguing to watch them come and go

Precious Moments

Words so simply spoken

We think are not retained

But when we're forced to memory

We find they were contained

Movements so simply gestured

We think so little of at all

But as time and life passes

From memory we can recall

Life and all it's beauty

So quickly passes by

And when it's taken from us

Our hearts break down and cry

All those precious moments

We no longer hear or see

But in our heart and memories

Real or Passing Moment

I fear of my insensitivity

For negligence can be the devastation

Think of me, not as cold

But with a loving heart

Barred only by respect

Yet unable to withstand

Return of such a trial

Is it easier to remain aloof

Or to give way to the quiet need

Did I pass or did I fail

I fear of my timidity

For who am I to gain such a treasure

Who am I to gain such life

Think of me, til the end of time

As one who loves you dearly

Barred only by distance

Yet unable to remove the vastness

Is it easier to remain afar

Or to bridge the silent yearning

Do I stir or do I stay

A struggle which presses the memory's heart.

Rising

I feel a cold rush over

Strange now how I feel

Memories flash before me

I know this wrong is real

I feel myself rising

And I see where I falter

But the light that shines before me

Saves me from deep water

I cannot hold you long enough

But I leave you with my love

And as I go before you

I'll wait for you above

Sheltered Beneath the Shield

One of such a fiery spirit

Unknown by those who see

But only he who looks beyond

Knows the beauty there might be

Intriguing to watch them move about

Waiting, anxious for them to slow

For sheltered beneath the outer shield

Is a heart with a gentle glow

If only time could then stand still

To absorb the moment's grace

One could then become enamored

By the softness behind the face

Signs of Life

Neglect not, the signs of spring

The beauty has it's season

As love too causes hearts to sing

And implores no rhyme or reason

Then sets the calm of summer

As all tends to sail

Hearts content with waves of laughter

And life seems to prevail

Then the changes come in autumn

As leaves begin to fall

Presenting with it's splendid color

The beauty changes all

Then begins the winds of winter

With it's harsh and bitter cold

Followed by thoughts to remember

Someday

Someday I will see

My sweet Jesus come for me

For someday I will be

In the place prepared for me

Oh the tears, stream down my face

As I sing Amazing Grace

Someday, some sweet day, I'll be home

As I look up at the clouds

I stand tall cause I'm so proud

My savior will call my name

When he comes for me to claim

Oh the tears, stream down my face

As I sing Amazing Grace

Someday, some sweet day, I'll be home

His arms are open wide

For those who believe and will not hide

Close your eyes and feel his touch

For he loves us oh so much

Oh the tears, stream down my face

As we sing Amazing Grace

Someday, some sweet day, we'll all be home

Strings to our Heart

There comes a time when someone we meet

Can pull the string to our heart

And given time along a daily path

Can make it so hard to part

Left to ponder upon the past

And thoughts of what could have been

If only some things could be done over

Now wondering if you'll meet again

Oh, if that day should come at last

What would the moment bring

Would things pick up from where they left

Or would it play to a different string

The Distant Light

I closed my eyes as if to sleep
As darkness filled the night
I was amazed at what I saw
For there shone a distant light

Closer I came, that I might see
To the hilltop on which to stand
It was no mistake, looking back at me
Was the angel's heavenly band

I saw in the midst a familiar face
Of one I had loved so dear
I had no idea my time had come
And the crowd began to cheer

One by one they all had gathered

To sing a welcome unto me

Then my friend took my hand

And so sweetly smiled at me

This beautiful land is a token

Of which Jesus held the key

And by my faith I had spoken

Now Jesus had remembered me

The Midnight Hour

Wakened in the midnight hour
My soul shuddered within me
Just to think if I should die
And Jesus were not with me

Such a sinner, so unworthy
Of the blood He shed for me
For all the years I turned my back
And simply refused to see

Oh that thought kept me awake
For I could no longer sleep
So to my knees I earnestly prayed
Dear Lord, my soul, please keep

He said my child, rise up and know
I would never turn away
When in your heart you've come home

The Midst of a Storm

Sinking in the midst of a storm
I felt I could no longer float
Then out of the darkness
Came a bright shining light
And I could see my dear savior's boat

Struggling in the waves of despair
I thought certain I'd drawn my last breath
Then an outstretched hand lifted me up
And saved me from a most certain death

I could see the scars in his gentle hands
And the love shone in his eyes
He calmed my sea as I called his name
Thank God he had heard my heart cries

With renewed strength and pardoned sins

I saw a tear had been on his face

Yes it was He, the one who had died

And saved my soul with amazing grace

So yes, I will tell the story

And I'll sing praises for what he did for me

And wait the day I shall see him in glory

And the place he's prepared for me

The Morning's Dawn

Oh that precious moment
As the morning's stillness lay
When the sun peeks over the horizon
And brings forth the light of day

I feel His presence surround me
And just takes my breath away
My heart so filled with gladness
I fall to my knees to pray

Weakened as it floods my soul
The tears find their way
Oh the power of that sweet feeling
When Jesus came in to stay

Lifted by his Holy Spirit

I no longer wish to stray

For someday I'll be lifted up

To a home so far away

There I shall live forever more

Oh what a glorious day

The Poet

Appearance has it, one is idle

Though busy in his thought

Who's to break the poet's bridle

Til he's found what he has sought

Shake him not from the moment

For his focus might be broken

Left to wonder what might be taught

Or words be left unspoken

The Storm Passes By

When troubles seem to surround you

Like the darkness in the night

When the storm hovers about you

And things just aren't so bright

When the clouds clap their thunder

And lightening strikes all about

Just praise your blessed Savior

And he'll turn your life about

When the burdens get too heavy

And it seems to weigh you down

When you need someone beside you

And there's just no one around

If you'll lift your voice to heaven

God will hear your prayer

There you'll find an answer

And know he's always there

When you give your heart to Jesus

Your life will be made new

No more to tread in darkness

He's already paid the due

When you open your heart to Jesus

He'll hear your beckoned cry

And wrap his arms around you

Til the storm cloud passes by

Then They Were Grown

Twice upon December nights

Precious babies were born

With curly hair and eyes so bright

Wrapped in cozy blankets warm

Joy filled the hearts of all

Of those who came to see

But words cannot express at all

What those tiny babies gave me

Cute little fingers and tiny toes

And a mind all their own

Together we loved, laughed and played

And then one day they were grown

We played football, basketball

Softball and soccer

They brought home pets

They thought we should keep

I said 'Oh Lord, it's time for my rocker

And now there's grandkids to keep'

Oh so cute when they look up and say

'Grandma, I love you'

So in my arms I give a big hug

And of course 'I love you too!'

Time

I lie awake and wish not to sleep

As morning comes too soon

I watch you breathe in slumber deep

In the stillness lit by the moon

The clock ticks on the bedside table

For time does not stand still

I treasure the moment while I'm able

And my heart's content shall fill

The sun will soon rise and shun the moon

To make course for another day

The hands of time come all too soon

And will take us both away

Tokens

The things I do

I have a reason

Doesn't matter the day

Or even the season

I don't want praise

Or any kind of glory

But behind all these things

There is a story

I've sat back and watched

Enough to know

Just what it is

That pleases you so

And these little things

Are just a token

Of feelings so deep

Unto You

Lord, the darkest cloud may come our way
But nothing can dim our view
We've planted our feet on solid ground
And sing our praises unto you

When all shall gather from the ends of earth
As the trumpet sounds 'it's due'
Lord we pray you'll find us ready
As we sing our praises unto you

When we hear the sound of such sweet singing
Then that choir we'll join too
Oh, how the joy in our hearts runneth over
As we sing our praises unto you

Values

Life seems so repetitious
As we go from day to day
At times it goes so slowly
That we wish our life away

Each step is just important
As it was the day before
And presents itself a challenge
As it opens up new doors

Looking back we can see
Importance we've been taught
Like how to place our values
On things that can't be bought

But the value of a person
Shouldn't be measured by house or car
Nor in the special gift they have
That's brought them through thus far

Those gifted with love and kindness
Is in the attitude that they show
That's what builds the character
And makes one's brighter glow

So don't judge by looks too quickly
But rather look within one's heart
The real gift might be the person
Don't miss this valuable part

What a Difference

Some were just meant to light the world
And what a difference they have made
When others would have turned away
With sacrifice they stayed

Some were meant to fill this world
With loyalty and compassion
Some seem to do it so well
In the highest form and fashion

Some were meant to make a difference
And are admired with great pride
For their selfless acts of courage
And the faithfulness they provide

What Jesus Said

Today I spoke with Jesus

He said, don't fret and worry

He said to simply bide my time

And not be in such a hurry

He said when I get hungry

To just keep Him in mind

Try not to falter

Then seek and I would find

He said when I get weary

Just call upon His name

He said he'd be beside me

For he could heal the lame

He said if I am troubled

Just believe in me

All it takes is faith

Then peace you will see

He said if I would serve Him

Doing good and faithful deeds

He would keep his promise

And supply all my needs

He said if I would love him

With all my heart and soul

He would send a comforter

That I would surely know

When

As I watch the sun rise

I wish you were beside me

As I watch the river rage

I remember your every touch

When did I come to love you so much?

Absence makes the heart grow fonder

Waiting for time to remove the loss

Distance makes the yearning stronger

While memories build a crutch

When did I come to love you so much?

Was it that moment when your eyes caught mine?

When I Fall Silent

Sometimes I may fall silent
As I listen to you speak
But all the while, my heart cries out
And to the Lord in prayer I seek

Sometimes I may fall silent
For I know not what to say
What words could be spoken
To make for a brighter day

Sometimes I may fall silent
While fighting back some tears
I've grown to love you oh so much
Throughout so many years

Sometimes I may fall silent
As I watch you and I know
Someday my heart will simply break

Will You

Will you share your love with others
And show them that you care
Will you give them some comfort
And love like what we share

Will you share in your laughter
And show your precious smile
Will you walk hand in hand together
And give that extra mile

Will you be there in their troubles
And give a helping hand
Will you help them to find Jesus
And make a lasting stand

Will you do these things in Jesus name
And remember it's by His grace
Will you teach them as we part this world

Who

Who do you confide in

when life gets you down?

Who do you seek

when no one is around?

Who's shoulder do you cry on

when you're feeling blue?

Who looks into your eyes

to see the real you?

Who makes you laugh

until you could cry?

Who loves you so much

and never asks why?

Who keeps you warm

on cold winter days?

Who loves you in spite

of imperfect ways?

Who loves you unconditionally

to never leave your side?

Who can you run to

with arms open wide?

Who sees your heart

your pain and desires?

Who gives you that touch

that sparks your internal fire?

Who do you love

that you'd never want to lose?

Who loves you back

who would you choose?

Words

You cannot take back

What has been said

So only speak

From the heart instead

Hateful words

Can cause such pain

Be careful of anger

And try to refrain

Once a heart

Has been broken

Those words can never

Be unspoken

It takes some time

To know one's heart

So don't let words

Tear you apart

Once words are said

You cannot relive

So be more careful

Of each moment you give

World of Beauty

As I stopped to smell the roses

With the fragrance in the air

I stop to think how very much

The Lord must really care

For a world so full of beauty

If only you care to see

It's just a portion of how much

God cares for you and me

For it's in the soft and gentle

Brushing of the wind

Or in the loving caring smile

Of a special friend

It's in a soft and gentle hug

Of some sweet precious child

Or in the deer across the field

Free and running wild

And as I stop to smell that rose

All these things come to mind

I'm so thankful for today

And each new gift I find.

Yesterday

It seems like only yesterday
You'd take me by the hand
And tell me some old stories
Of a far away land

You'd set me on your lap to tell me
Of some magnificent place
I remember the sparkle in your eye
And the smile upon your face

It seems like only yesterday
But as I look at you today
Your walk has gotten much slower
Your hair has turned to gray

I still watch you tell your stories

Though I'm too big now for your knee

I wonder if you realize

How much you mean to me

Yes, it seems like only yesterday

And not so long ago

But as life rushes on I wonder

Where did the time seem to go?

Young Once

Babies become toddlers

And learn to tie their shoe

I can still remember

I was young once too

Toddlers become children

And throw a fit or two

I can still remember

I was young once too

Children become adults

And have so much to do

Sometimes they forget

That they were young once too

Adults just get older

Get gray and wrinkles too

Then they sit and ponder